For Ethan and Zuri

Illustrated by Jen Fuller

TORTY SINGS THE DIRGE

by Ms. Ken

*O*nce upon a long time ago in Animasia, the old Queen Agunia's spirit left her shell and departed on the journey to Alamuo, the eternal resting place of all spirits.

In Animasia, on the fourteenth day after a royal animal died, the animals would choose someone to sing a dirge, a song that would open the doors of Alamuo to the departed spirit. There would be a singing contest, and everyone was welcome to try.

It was a great honor in Animasia to be chosen as the dirge singer. The animal would get to ride on King Agu's royal stool for a whole day, carried by the four royal hyenas, and be treated to all kinds of delicacies. He would also be made a member of the Nze, the King's royal advisers.

Torty was determined to sing the dirge no matter what it took. There was, however, one small problem. Torty couldn't sing a word. Still, he was going to find a way

On the seventh day after Queen Agunia died, the sun roused all the animals from their sleep and warmed the water in the stream for their morning baths. After breakfast, the animals gathered under the old baobab tree to try out to be Queen Agunia's dirge singer.

4

The elephants were present, noisily chewing on bamboo stalks.
The tigers sat beside their cousins the cheetahs, chatting. The
monkeys swung noisily from one branch of the baobab tree to the
other, startling the squirrels who twitched nervously, flicking their
bushy tails.

Cricky, the lonely cricket who lived in the thicket, was there
perched up on a leaf, where no one noticed him. Below him sat
Torty, still thinking of what he could do to win the contest.

Parry flew onto Elder's head where everyone could see him and
cleared his throat. He began importantly, "Noble animals of
Animasia, we all know the sad reason we are here this evening."
The animals chorused a sad sigh.

"May the soul of our departed queen depart in peace."
"Mena!" the animals answered.
"May her journey to the world beyond the skies be free of
troubles."
"Mena!" they answered again.
"May the chosen dirge singer open the gates of Alamuo with..."
"Wait!"
All eyes turned to Torty, who had interrupted Parry's speech.

"Yes, Torty?" Parry asked patiently.

So Torty continued, "The thing is this: we know that our Queen's entry into Alamuo will be determined by the dirge singer's ability to impress the gods. Well, I have an idea that would help us choose the perfect singer. We have another week before we must choose the dirge singer, right?"

"Right, Torty, but please could you speak a bit faster?" answered Elder, swinging his huge trunk.

"Let all animals return to their homes and brush up on their singing. After one week, we all come together again and then choose the best singer."

The animals started to speak at once, arguing about Torty's strange idea. They hadn't heard anything like it before. You either knew how to sing or you didn't, period!

Wise Parry sat silent, considering the idea. When he had almost worn himself out with considering, he flapped his well-pruned feathers to get the attention of the chattering animals, who were all consumed with this annoying idea of practicing for a week.

Finally, Elder raised his enormous trunk and let out a frightening "Harroooomphhh!"

At once, the animals fell silent, and Parry proceeded. "I say we take a vote. Those who agree with Torty's idea, move to my right. Those who do not agree, move to my left."

There was a lot of noise and shuffling as the animals hurried from left to right and from right to left. There were yelps and shouts of pain and anger as some of the smaller animals were trampled upon by the larger ones. Finally, after they had all settled, those on Parry's right far outnumbered those on his left. Torty had won.

"We meet again one week after today to choose our singer," Parry announced with a flap of his wings, and the meeting closed. The animals dispersed in a racket as they chatted with much excitement about who the singer was going to be.

"It could be no other but me," boasted Melodia, the proud nightingale. "We all know there is no finer singer than I in all of Animasia!"

"Oh, but my voice is the strongest and can be heard for miles and miles away!" Mrs. Ellie Elder trumpeted.

The only quiet ones were Cricky and Torty. Cricky was too shy to argue with the other animals, so he just hopped on home. Torty, on the other hand, was so engrossed with his plan that he did not feel like talking.

As the days passed and the animals practiced, the jungle experienced not a single quiet moment. Rats and bats squealed, insects chirped, elephants trumpeted, and goats bleated. Cats meowed, frogs croaked, horses neighed, and snakes hissed.

Oh, what a cacophony they made! But guess what?

Old Torty did not make a sound. No. He did not practice a single note. Instead, he spent the time sneaking from one animal's house to the other, eavesdropping on their singing, trying to find the best singer.

As he was spying on Melodia the nightingale, Torty thought, "Now I just have to find a way to steal her lovely voice." He hadn't even finished thinking it when he heard the most marvelous singing coming from somewhere close by.

He followed the sound of the voice, and it led him to a tiny window. He wiped some grime off the window and stuck his nose closer until he could see clearly into a neat little room. There, on a green Ugu leaf, sat shy, quiet Cricky, singing as though his tiny heart would burst.

He was singing about his lonely life with no friends or family. He sang about how bold he was going to be someday, about having many friends and maybe becoming part of a family in Animasia.

After Torty wiped some tears off his face, he grinned. He suddenly had an idea that did not involve stealing anyone's voice. "Oh better, much better," he said. "Now all I have to do is convince our Cricky here into making an agreement with me."

"Ooya, Cricky, are you home?"

Immediately, the singing stopped, and the cricket peeped to see who was visiting him. It was so unusual; he never had any visitors. He didn't even think anyone remembered that he existed at all. "Oh hel..lo, Mr. Torty..." stammered Cricky.

"May I come in, Crick? And please, call me Torty." But Torty was already pushing his way into the room.

"I came to see how you are getting on with your singing practice and maybe help you if you don't mind."

Cricky was flattered, to say the least, to be visited by such an important animal. "Why...well, Mr...erm Torty...why, that's kind of you..."

"So here's the plan, Crick. I'm going to help you become a star. You deserve to be heard by all. You will practice singing every day. I will come around often to supervise you, of course.

"On the day of the funeral, you will hide in the pocket of my robe since you are quite shy, and you will sing in your sweetest, most melodious voice."

"I will face the crowd while you sing. Each time I tap my pocket twice, you begin singing. When I tap once, you stop singing. Okay? After everything is done, I will introduce you to the crowd."

Cricky nodded numbly. He couldn't understand what was going on, but he somehow knew this was the break he had been waiting for.

"Trust me, Crick, I'm going to make you famous. You'll have so

many friends and admirers you won't know what to do with them."
And Torty left, with a huge grin on his face.

For the rest of that day, Cricky chirped and sang happy tunes.
He thought of all the friends he was going to make and went to bed
smiling. Cricky would finally be noticed and loved by all.

The day of the competition dawned bright and clear. All the
animals gathered again under the baobab tree in beautiful clothes.
Torty wore a long, flowing robe that had a big pocket on the side.
Snuggled deep in the pocket was a very nervous Cricky.

Parry scratched his claws together, the signal for the
competition to begin. First up were the Elephants. They trumpeted
long and loud and gave everyone a headache. The bees buzzed
when it was their turn. The mice squealed impressively, the horses
neighed, and the birds chirped sweetly.

Then, Melodia the nightingale opened her beak and sang out
in her beautiful voice. All the animals clapped wildly. They were sure
they had heard the best singing in Animasia. Ikwikwi the owl, chosen
to be the judge, stepped on stage to declare the winner.

At that moment, Torty strutted forward
and placed a hand on Ikwikwi's shoulder.
"Hold on, brother. I haven't had my turn yet."

"Oh Torty, please spare us. Even Grizzly sings better than you do!"

The animals laughed. Torty ignored them and
waited patiently until everyone was
quiet again. He cleared his throat
and tapped his pocket twice.
He opened his mouth and
moved it right as Cricky's
sweet and piercing
voice filled the air.

A hush fell on Animasia. The animals could not believe their ears! They had never thought that Torty, of all creatures, could sing, but the music was so beautiful that there was not a dry eye in the crowd.

Torty tapped his pocket once to let Cricky know it was time to stop. "We pick Torty, we pick Torty!" the animals cried when it was time for the judges to decide. Even Melodia agreed.

Once again, Ikwikwi climbed the stage to declare the winner. He adjusted his glasses and peered at the leaf in his hand. He cleared his throat. "Our dirge singer is Torty!"

Poor Cricky! He was very confused. Torty had promised to make him famous, but instead, Torty was the one getting all the cheers. "I'll just wait until everything cools down, and maybe Torty will explain things," Cricky thought.

Later, a very happy Torty safely deposited a very sad Cricky in his little hole in the mango tree. "Look, Cricky," he explained. "I see no reason for you to be sad. As your manager, it's quite natural for me to get some recognition first."

"I promise that after the funeral, everything will be alright." And the trusting little cricket believed him.

Finally, the funeral day arrived, and all the animals in Animasia gathered in the Forest of Bones, the burial place of all animals. The animals wore dark colors and sad, long faces. Enweocha, the old, grayed monkey that lived beyond the seven mountains, led the ceremony.

After a speech about the virtues of the late queen, he got to the part that everyone had been waiting for.

"...and we commit our great Queen Agunia to mother earth, from where she shall proceed to the ancestral home of Alamuo. The dirge, please."

Torty strutted proudly to the center of the stage and took his position on the great stump. He tapped his pocket twice, and Cricky's melodious voice filled the air once again, bringing all the animals to tears. The animals shouted, "More, more!" Torty tapped his pocket twice again, and once more, Cricky's voice rang out over the hushed forest.

Cheers for Torty rose into the air, and calls for more went up again and again and again. Poor Cricky! He was very tired by this time and could barely raise his voice. After all, crickets are fragile creatures. He had not eaten nor drank anything all day, and the heat was getting to him, being squashed as he was in Torty's pocket.

Meanwhile, Torty was having all the fun - food and drinks were brought up to him after every performance. He was the toast of the occasion. Cricky tried to tell him how tired and hungry he was, but Torty ignored him.

When the next song started, the animals noticed that Torty's voice, or at least the voice they thought was Torty's, had become weak and strained. Torty tapped his pocket again after that song was finished, but our poor Cricky had had enough. He flew out of Torty's pocket and landed on the stage with a thud. Slowly and with his fading strength, he started to sing one last song.

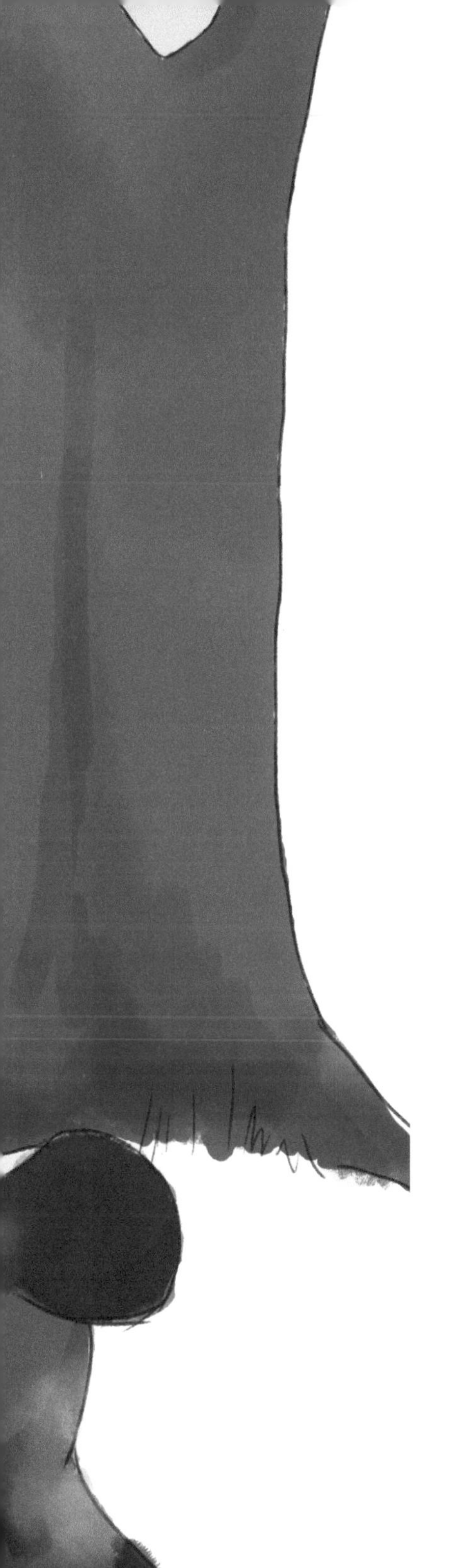

I am a lonely cricket
With no father or mother
I live up in the thicket
Just me and no other

Torty said he'd make me famous
He said I'd have lots of friends
That my wealth would be enormous
Much more than I could spend

I am a little chirper
I chirp all day and night
But I'd be much happier
To shine out in the light

There was a deep hush while Cricky sang his song. All the animals were astonished. "Down with Torty, up with Cricky!" they yelled at last. Immediately, the angry animals lifted up the tortoise and threw him out beyond the Forest of Bones.

His smooth, shiny shell, which he had painstakingly polished only that morning, cracked in a hundred places. And that is exactly how the tortoise came to have a rough, patched shell.

As for the cricket, he got to ride on King Agu's royal stool for a whole day, carried by the four royal hyenas, and was treated to all kinds of delicacies.

He also became the village singer, and he was given a place as an honored member of the Nze. Of course, he was never lonely in his thicket again.

29

www.ingramcontent.com/pod-product-compliance
Lightning Source LLC
Chambersburg PA
CBHW042014110726
48006CB00004B/1084